Futurekids

THE INTERNET EXPEDITION

By Ron Harris and Lil' Gangster

Original Story by Ron Harris and David Ullendorff

ZIFF-DAVIS
ZD
PRESS

The Lil' Gangster Art Team:
Ron Harris: Script, pencils, inking, color, digital assembly
Romeo Francisco, Cesar Magsombol, Paul de Leon: Inking
424 Studios: Digital color
Byron Virula: Background Inking, production assistance
Joey Harris: Production assistance
Gangster Production, Paris: Original character designs

The Ziff-Davis Press Editorial and Production Team:
Dan Brodnitz: Development Editor
Ami Knox: Project Coordinator
Tony Jonick: Prepress-Layout Mechanic
Joe Schneider: Prepress-Color Correction Specialist

Ziff-Davis Press books are produced on a Macintosh computer system with the following applications: FrameMaker®, Microsoft® Word, QuarkXPress®, Adobe Illustrator®, Adobe Photoshop®, Adobe Streamline™, MacLink® *Plus*, Aldus® FreeHand™, Collage Plus™.

If you have comments or questions or would like to receive a free catalog, call or write:
Ziff-Davis Press
5903 Christie Avenue
Emeryville, CA 94608
1-800-688-0448

If you would like to learn more about Futurekids, Inc., contact:
Futurekids
5777 West Century Blvd.
Suite 1555
Los Angeles, California 90045
310-337-7006

ISBN 1-56276-271-0

Manufactured in the United States of America
10 9 8 7 6 5 4 3 2 1

ON FOUR CONTINENTS, GLEAMING ROCKETS STAND READY. THEY ARE THE LATEST STRANDS OF A COMMUNICATIONS WEB THAT COVERS THE GLOBE...

FRANCE REPORTS READY.

JAPAN REPORTS READY.

IN THE CONTROL CENTERS, THE AIR IS TENSE WITH EXCITEMENT. IN THE WORLD OUTSIDE, BORED BY TOO MANY SATELLITE LAUNCHINGS, NOBODY PAYS MUCH ATTENTION...

EXCEPT IN **ONE** UNLIKELY SPOT. IN A SQUALID NEIGHBORHOOD ON THE OUTSKIRTS OF A LARGE MEXICAN CITY, A CERTAIN GIRL FOLLOWS THE LAUNCH WITH KEEN EXCITEMENT...

TWO AGAINST ONE IS NO FAIR!

LET'S GET GABRIELA TO EVEN THINGS UP.

...all four satellites will take off at the same time, completing a global information network that...

HEY, GABRIELA! TAKE A BREAK AND PLAY FOOTBALL WITH US!

NO WAY! THIS IS IMPORTANT!

WITH UNLIMITED INTERNET ACCESS, I CAN SPREAD THE ROSS McHUGH ENTREPRENEUR NETWORK AROUND THE WORLD!

I CAN RESELL OBSOLETE SOFTWARE TO CHINA!

HUSTLE NEW INVESTORS FOR MY BUSINESS VENTURES!

TARO

Taro here. It's a peaceful night by Ise Bay. In the distance I can just see the shadow of Mount Kamiji...will linking up by satellite really help us?

CLAUDE

Claude in Paris. Yes! It'll be like living next door to each other.

GABRIELA

Once we're hooked into the satellites, we'll have a free permanent link between us. Then we can find other kids to join us, and start our own community.

GABRIELA

The satellites will be in orbit in twenty minutes. Then I'll send my signal!

BRAZIL REPORTS LIFTOFF!

TARO

Connections and inter-connections. I wonder if the world can become TOO well connected.

FRANCE REPORTS LIFTOFF!

HEY, BENNY. T-SHIRT IDEA. "I GOT GRIDLOCKED ON THE INFORMATION SUPERHIGHWAY."

"WE GET GUYS TO PEDDLE THEM BY THE FREEWAY RAMPS. WHAT D'YOU SAY—MAKE ME 1,500 SHIRTS ON CREDIT AND I'LL CUT YOU IN FOR HALF."

"COME ON! I WANT TO GET SOMETHING OUT OF THIS SATELLITE LAUNCH."

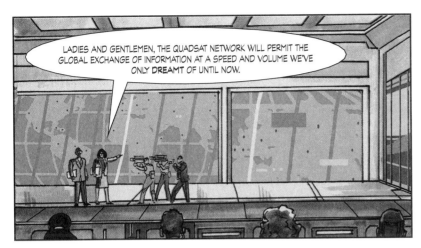

NO! LET ME GO!

H-HELP!!

THOUGHT SO. IT WAS THAT BEAT-UP POWER SUPPLY I DUG UP FROM THE ARMY DUMP.

THIS WORK-AROUND SHOULD HOLD FOR A FEW HOURS—I THINK.

HOPE THE OTHERS DIDN'T GIVE UP ON ME.

CLAUDE
There you are, Gabriela. Both you and Ross went off-line together.

TARO
Does it have something to do with this strange window?

IT MUST. WHATEVER IT IS, THAT WINDOW APPEARED JUST WHEN I LINKED UP WITH THE SATELLITES.

FUNNY. THOSE SYMBOLS LOOK LIKE COORDINATES.

THEY CHANGE AS I MOVE THE MOUSE. AND SO DOES THE PICTURE!

IT'S LIKE I'M FLYING A CAMERA PLANE THROUGH THE UNIVERSE!

THIS INCREDIBLE FULL-MOTION VIDEO IS SO SHARP IT LOOKS REAL!

ONLY THING IS, MY MONITOR SHOULDN'T BE ABLE TO DISPLAY GRAPHICS LIKE THIS...

...NOT TO MENTION MY COMPUTER!

ULP! IT'S ME!

I MEAN, IT'S A PICTURE OF ME, LYING ON A TABLE.

THAT'S THE FAKE PICTURE I SENT TO MY NETMATES.

I'LL TRY TO ZOOM OUT...

I RECOGNIZE THAT ROOM! IT'S THE ONE IN ROSS'S PICTURE!

THIS IS BEYOND WEIRD. IT'S ALMOST SCARY!

CLAUDE
That's ridiculous!

TARO
I'm no technical expert, Gabriela, but I know enough to tell you monitors don't work that way.

GABRIELA
But it's true! I was really in Ross's room!

THEY'VE **GOT** TO BELIEVE ME!

GABRIELA
I'm certain somebody kidnapped him and took him through that window.

CLAUDE
Talk sense, Gabriela. This whole window thing is a joke you're playing on us, right?

GABRIELA
Joke, huh? Just click on the window and type these coordinates.

HA! WAIT'LL CLAUDE SEES THIS! I BET HE'LL CHANGE HIS—

HUH? WHO'S THAT?

CLAUDE
Gabriela, it's **you!** Or at least, it **looks** sort of like you.

HEY! WHAT'D YOU DO WITH CLAUDE?!

YAAH!

WHY, THIS IS A GIRL'S ROOM!

YOU'RE CLAUDE— AND YOU'RE A FAKE!

...SO I'M SURE SOMEONE ON THE OTHER SIDE OF THE WINDOW TOOK ROSS *PRISONER.* HE MAY EVEN BE HURT.

IF I HADN'T SEEN YOU ARRIVE, I'D SAY YOU WERE *CRAZY.* BUT HERE YOU ARE— AND I'M NOT CRAZY.

I THINK.

ANYWAY, WE HAVE TO *RESCUE* HIM!

YOUR BATTERIES, GREGOIRE.

CLAUDE, DON'T FOR- GET YOU HAVE TO DO YOUR BROTHER'S LAUNDRY TONIGHT.

MOTHER, THERE'S THAT GIRL AGAIN. SHE DOESN'T LIVE HERE, DOES SHE?

WHAT? I CAN'T HEAR YOU, GREGOIRE.

WE CAN USE THE WINDOW TO GO GET TARO.

SOUNDS LIKE WE'D BETTER BE PREPARED.

THEN WE'LL INPUT THE COORDINATES ROSS USED.

WHAT'S THAT? SURVIVAL GEAR?

WE NEVER KNOW WHAT WE'LL RUN INTO. LET'S CONTACT TARO.

TARO

There you are, Gabriela. I wondered where you went.

GABRIELA

I hopped through the monitor to Claude's place. I'm in Paris now.

TARO

You made this joke before, Gabriela. I'm afraid you'll have to prove it to me.

GABRIELA

Just stand back and wait a few seconds.

I'VE ALWAYS WANTED TO VISIT JAPAN. IT'S SO SERENE. REMEMBER THE PICTURE HE SENT?

TIMELESS ISE—WHERE ONE STILL FINDS THE PEACE AND BEAUTY OF OLD JAPAN. THE SORT OF PLACE ONE WOULD FIND ON A POSTCARD...

...WHICH IS EXACTLY WHERE TARO FOUND THE PICTURE...

WHAT?!!

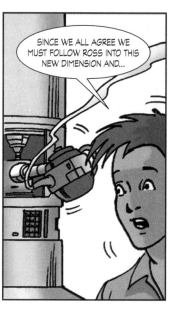

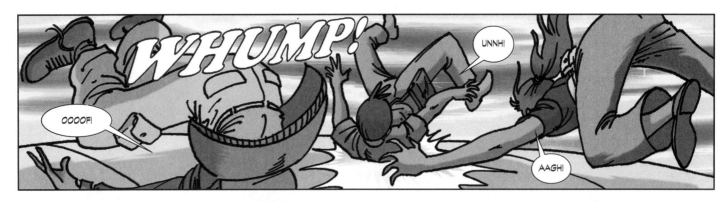

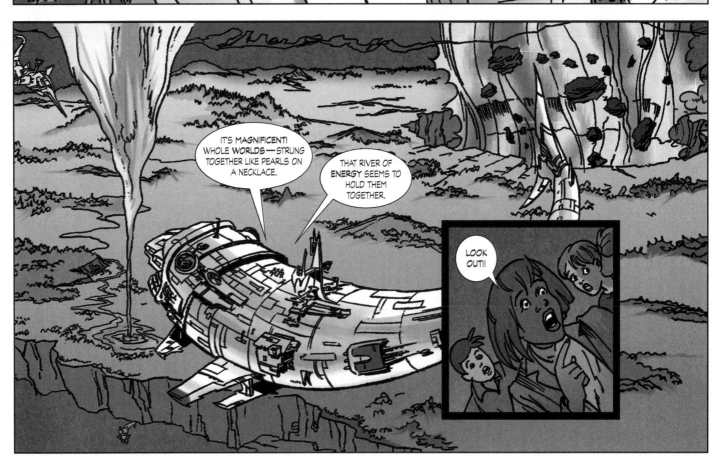

OWW! THAT AWFUL SOUND!

THE CLOSER THEY GET, THE STRONGER IT BECOMES!

HOW CAN WE FIGHT BACK?

THEY'RE ALL AROUND US... NOISE...SO LOUD...

STRANGE...CAN'T HEAR WORDS...BUT I HEAR...THEIR FEELINGS...

IT SOUNDS LIKE...

...FEAR!

IT IS, MY FRIENDS.

THE NOISE OF YOUR ARRIVAL UPSET THEM TERRIBLY.

THEY CAN'T SEE YOU, OF COURSE, SO THEY CAN ONLY JUDGE BY WHAT THEY HEAR...

THEY SEEM TO BE CALMING DOWN.

I TOLD THEM THEY'RE IN NO DANGER. THAT'S WHAT WE HARMONIZERS ARE FOR, AFTER ALL.

THAT'S WHAT YOU ARE—A HARMONIZER?

OF COURSE! LET'S GO OVER THERE TO TALK.

THE GURGLING OF AIR CURRENTS AROUND TALL TALKING OBJECTS IS PARTICULARLY DISTRESSING TO THEM.

HOLD STILL SO I CAN DRAW YOU.

YOU DRAW! I DO SO MISS THE ARTS. THE CENTRANS LEFT ME HERE A LONG TIME AGO AND, WELL, YOU KNOW THESE DAYS...

NOT THAT THE ZANORANS AREN'T WONDERFUL BEINGS. I JUST MISS ALL THE VISITORS WE HAD BEFORE THE FLUX FILLED UP...

THE FREE TRADERS NEVER STOP ON ZANORA.

CENTRANS? FLUX? FREE TRADERS? WHAT ARE YOU TALKING ABOUT?

YOU DON'T KNOW ABOUT THE **FLUX**? WHERE ARE YOU **FROM**?

LET'S JUST SAY WE CAME FROM A LONG WAY OFF.

THE FLUX IS, WELL, WHY, IT'S THE CENTER OF **EVERYTHING**, ISN'T IT?

IT'S THE FORCE THAT BINDS THE CORE WORLDS TOGETHER. AND IT'S THE ONLY EASY WAY TO TRAVEL BETWEEN THE DIFFERENT WORLDS.

AT LEAST, IT **USED** TO BE.

PLEASE HOLD YOUR HEAD STILL!

THERE WAS COMMERCE ONCE. AH, WHAT GREAT TIMES! FLEETS OF MIGHTY SHIPS CARRIED GOODS AROUND ALL THE CORE WORLDS.

THEN SOMETHING TERRIBLE HAPPENED.

THE CORE WORLDS BEGAN TO **CRUMBLE**. CHUNKS OF DEBRIS FILLED THE FLUX, THREATENING THE SHIPS.

SOON ONLY THE BRAVEST—OR SHOULD I SAY, THE MOST **FOOLHARDY**—TRADERS WOULD RISK SAILING THE FLUX.

THE MANY WORLDS **LOST** TOUCH.

I CAME LONG AGO FROM THE CENTER, THE FINEST WORLD OF ALL. THE **CENTRANS** BUILT ME. AH, I MISS IT SO.

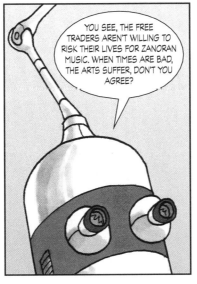

YOU SEE, THE FREE TRADERS AREN'T WILLING TO RISK THEIR LIVES FOR ZANORAN MUSIC. WHEN TIMES ARE BAD, THE ARTS SUFFER, DON'T YOU AGREE?

A FRIEND OF OURS DISAPPEARED INTO THE CORE WORLDS. IT'S A LONG STORY.

ANYWAY, WE DON'T KNOW WHERE TO START LOOKING FOR HIM.

WHY, I'D START AT THE **CENTER**, OF COURSE. THE CENTRANS ARE THINKERS—**DOERS**! IF ANYONE KNOWS HOW TO FIND YOUR FRIEND, **THEY** DO.

YES, START AT THE CENTER—IF YOU CAN GET THERE, THAT IS.

I'M NOT MUCH HELP ON **THAT** SCORE, I'M AFRAID.

I'D LIKE TO SEE THE FLUX. CAN YOU SHOW IT TO US?

WHEW! WE MADE IT TO THE FIRST STEP. NOW LET'S MAKE THE **NEXT**. AND THE NEXT AGAIN, UNTIL WE'RE THERE.

I'LL MISS THE HARMONIZER. I WANT TO SEE HIM AGAIN SOME DAY.

LOOK AT THOSE ODD INSECTLIKE THINGS. THEY ALMOST SEEM TO BE **EATING** THE ROCK.

YES, THERE ARE A MILLION WONDERS HERE. BUT WE DON'T HAVE TIME TO LOOK AT THEM ALL.

EVERY HOUR THAT PASSES MAY BE THE LAST IN ROSS'S LIFE!

TO ROSS McHUGH...LONG LIFE!

THIS IS A PRETTY IMPRESSIVE PLACE YOU'VE GOT HERE, PRESIDENT.

IT'S THE FINEST BUILDING IN THE CENTER, ROSS...

...A FITTING PLACE TO WELCOME THE FIRST VISITOR FROM ANOTHER DIMENSION.

YOU KNOW SO MUCH ABOUT YOUR HOME WORLD. YOU MUST TELL US EVERYTHING.

WELL, I DON'T KNOW **EVERYTHING**...

BUT I CAN PROBABLY TELL YOU ANYTHING YOU'D NEED TO KNOW.

NOW ABOUT THESE "TRADING CARDS..."

DINOMECHAZOIDS.

YOUR PEOPLE MUST HAVE INCREDIBLE TECHNOLOGY TO CREATE SUCH MACHINES!

OH, THESE PIX AREN'T EXACTLY...

UH, THAT IS, IF YOU LIKE 'EM I CAN EXPORT 'EM TO YOU IN BULK. THEY'RE BIG **SELLERS** BACK HOME.

LET ME SHOW YOU SOMETHING **OUR** ENGINEERS ARE VERY PROUD OF.

THEY SEEM TO BE HARVESTING THE FRUIT.

LET'S CATCH UP WITH THEM. THEY MAY BE ABLE TO HELP US.

GRAB ALL YOU CAN, BUT DON'T STOP MOVING. HURRY!

HEY THERE! CAN YOU HELP US OUT?

WHO ARE YOU? YOU'RE NOT BLEAKERS.

WE'RE STRANGERS. WE'RE TRYING TO GET TO THE CENTER.

HA! EVERYONE WOULD LIKE TO GET TO THE CENTER.

YOU MUST GO UP FOR THAT, STRANGERS. WAY UP.

CAN'T WASTE TIME CHATTING! WE'RE READY TO START ON THE VINES.

THE VINES ARE SWAYING. A STORM MUST BE RISING.

STORM? YOU STAY HERE AND YOU'LL SEE A STORM!

VINE HARVESTING TIME! LET'S MOVE!

WHACK

EEY!!!!

WHAT ARE YOU WAITING FOR? RUN!

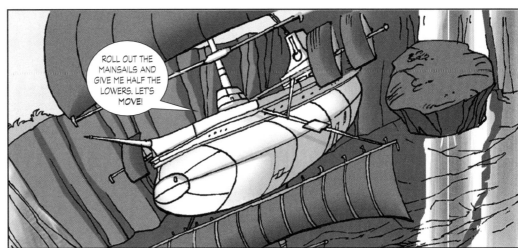

IT'S BEAUTIFUL! THE MIGHTIEST RIVERS ON EARTH ARE TINY COMPARED TO THIS!

THE CURRENT IS FASTEST IN THE MIDDLE OF THE FLUX, SO THAT'S WHERE THE CAPTAIN WANTS TO SAIL.

BUT THAT'S ALSO WHERE THE CHUNKS ARE THE THICKEST.

COLLAPSE THE PORT MIDSAILS!

DODGING THEM IS HARD AND DANGEROUS WORK.

HEEL TO STARBOARD AND ROLL OUT HALF TRIM! THERE'S A BIG ONE COMING!

IT'S TUMBLING! THREE POINTS DOWN AND DO IT FAST!

FAST, I SAID!

WE MISSED THE BIG 'UN, CAP'N, BUT WE TOOK A SMALL HIT IN THE NUMBER FOURTEEN TRIM!

WHOP!

THEN FIX IT! WE NEED EVERY PIECE OF SAIL WE'VE GOT!

SURVIVING VYNLAND IS ONLY HALF THE CHALLENGE. WE CAN'T REST UNTIL WE'RE SAFELY BACK TO THE BLEAK.

HA! IF YOU CALL THAT BEING SAFE.

THERE YOU ARE! COME ON, CAP'N SAYS YOU THREE WORK FOR YOUR RIDE!

I'M GETTING TO LIKE THIS PLACE! THEY APPRECIATE A GUY WITH THE COMPETITIVE SPIRIT!

AND THEIR DESIGN SENSE IS PURE LATE 50'S CLASSIC.

I COULD CLEAN OUT THE THRIFT STORES BACK HOME...RESELL THAT OLD FURNITURE HERE. I'D MAKE A FORTUNE.

OH, IT'S YOU, TREZZ. COME ON IN.

THE CORPORATE PRESIDENT IS WAITING FOR US, ROSS. BUT BEFORE I TAKE YOU TO HER I WANT YOU TO HAVE **THIS**.

ITS A PHYGGE XT PESONAL DATA MANAGER...THE LATEST MODEL.

WOW! THIS MAKES THE LAPTOPS BACK HOME LOOK **LAME!**

IT'S MY APOLOGY FOR **SHOOTING** AT YOU.

THAT WAS NO WAY TO **HONOR** A GUEST FROM ANOTHER DIMENSION.

THANKS, TREZZ. BUT NOW I UNDERSTAND WHY YOU WERE **AFRAID** OF ME. YOUR CENTRAN **WEAPONS** LOOK JUST LIKE AN EARTHSIDE MOUSE!

MOUSE?

A...POINTING DEVICE.

THEY WERE NAMED AFTER THESE ANIMALS BACK HOME. LITTLE THINGS THAT PEOPLE KEEP AS PETS.

I DON'T UNDERSTAND. WHAT ARE "PETS?"

YOU GUYS DON'T HAVE **PETS?**

THEY'RE ANIMALS THAT PEOPLE HAVE IN THEIR HOMES TO KEEP THEM COMPANY. THEY'RE REALLY POPULAR WHERE I COME FROM.

RABBITS, F'INSTANCE. CUTE, CUDDLY THINGS. HERE, LET ME SHOW YOU.

HOW D'YOU DRAW WITH THIS?

JUST MOVE YOUR FINGER.

WELL... I DON'T KNOW...

TELL YOU WHAT. I'LL GIVE YOU A PAIR OF RABBITS FREE OF CHARGE. TRY 'EM FOR 30 DAYS. SHOW 'EM TO OTHER CENTRANS.

IF YOU DON'T AGREE RABBITS ARE THE NEXT **SALES SENSATION**, RETURN THEM TO ME. YOU OWE NOTHING!

BUT IF YOU FIND — AS I THINK YOU WILL — THAT RABBITS ARE THE KEY TO BIG **PROFITS** AND FINANCIAL **SECURITY**, THEN KEEP THEM. ALL YOU OWE ME IS A SMALL ROYALTY ON ANY OFFSPRING.

YOU NEVER HAVE TO PAY FOR THE RABBITS THEMSELVES. THEY'RE MY OWN GIFT — TO YOU.

I'LL HAVE TO THINK IT OVER...

OKAY, TREZZ, BUT DON'T WAIT TOO LONG. ONLY A FEW RABBITS ARE AVAILABLE FOR EXPORT! DON'T MISS OUT ON THIS FANTASTIC OPPORTUNITY!

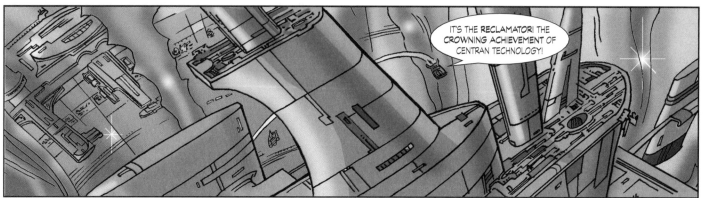

NOT UNLESS YOU WANT TO SPEND THE REST OF YOUR LIFE **SWIMMING** WITH THE ROCKS IN THE FLUX!

THAT'S INTERESTING. THOSE INSECTS ARE ON THE FLOATING CHUNKS, TOO.

THE CAPTAIN WANTS TO TALK TO YOU.

ACCORDING TO YOUR FRIEND HERE, YOU THINK WE'RE TAKING THOSE KIDS WITH US WHEN WE LEAVE.

BUT THAT'S WHAT YOU **PROMISED.** YOU SAID YOU'D TAKE THEM TO THE CENTER.

I SAID I'D TAKE THEM **AWAY** FROM VYNLAND. WELL, THEY'RE AWAY.

THE CENTER'S A LONG WAY FROM HERE, AND I DON'T NEED **CHARITY CASES** FOULING UP MY WEIGHTS AND BALANCES.

THEY STAY.

I **TOLD** YOU. THEY'RE OFF-WORLDERS. THEY CAN'T SURVIVE IN THE BLEAK.

WHY NOT? PEOPLE HAVE SURVIVED IN THE BLEAK FOR A LONG TIME. LOOK AT YOU GUYS.

WHEN I GO, THEY DON'T. END OF DISCUSSION.

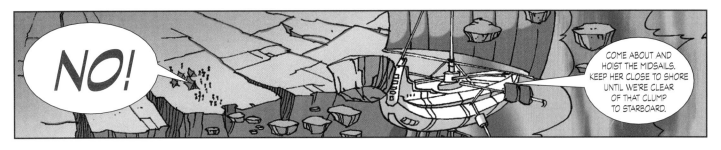

WHAT IN BLAZES ARE YOU DOING HERE?!

LIKE WE SAID, WE NEED A RIDE TO THE **CENTER**.

YOU HAVE TWO WAYS TO GET RID OF US, CAP'N. YOU CAN **TURN AROUND** AND TAKE US BACK TO THE **BLEAK**...

...OR YOU CAN **TOSS US OVERBOARD**.

NEITHER ONE IS **GOOD BUSINESS**, IS IT?

WHY YOU...I OUGHTA...

ZHLUBB! TAKE 'EM FORWARD AND PUT 'EM TO WORK!

BUT I'LL GET MY TROUBLE'S WORTH OUT OF YOU, BLAST IT! YOU'LL WORK **TWICE** AS HARD THIS TIME!

FOR HALF THE RATIONS!

HMMPH. YOU HAVE A LOT OF **COURAGE**, GIRL. I'LL GRANT YOU THAT.

(GRUMBLE!) I'M GONNA LOSE SO MUCH MONEY THIS TRIP...

IT SEEMS LIKE WE'VE SAILED FOR DAYS!

I WONDER HOW MANY WORLDS WE PASS BEFORE WE REACH THE CENTER.

HUH? NONE! THE CENTER IS OUR NEXT PORT.

BUT YOU TOLD US THE CENTER WAS A LONG WAY.

IT IS IF YOU'RE CARRYING NONPAYING PASSENGERS.

WHY DID THE BLEAKERS TELL US WE'D HAVE TO CLIMB WAY UP TO REACH THE CENTER?

HMMPH! SOME PEOPLE THINK UP IS THE ONLY WAY TO GET ANYWHERE.

YOU COULD WORK YOUR WAY UP-FLUX TOWARD THE CENTER. YOU'D PROBABLY GET THERE, EVENTUALLY.

BUT YOU'D BE OLD, TIRED, AND BROKE BY THE TIME YOU DID.

YOU TELL 'EM, MAP.

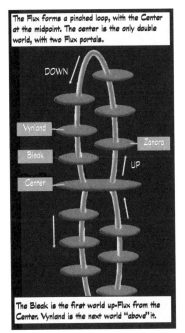

The Flux forms a pinched loop, with the Center at the midpoint. The center is the only double world, with two Flux portals.

DOWN

Vynland

Bleak

Center

Zanora

UP

The Bleak is the first world up-Flux from the Center. Vynland is the next world "above" it.

THEN HOW COULD WE CLIMB UP TO VYNLAND INSTEAD OF DOWN?

Many worlds overlap those on the opposite Flux stream. Vines and roots connecting the worlds make it possible to climb up to reach a down-Flux world.

Vynland

Zanora

THEN THE BLEAKERS ARE ONLY ONE WORLD AWAY FROM THE PLENTY THEY DESIRE.

AND YOU'VE NEVER TOLD THEM.

ARE YOU KIDDING?

IF THOSE GUYS GOT SOME IMAGINATION, I'D BE OUT OF THE ORE BUSINESS FAST!

I'VE GOT A LIVING TO EARN, KID!

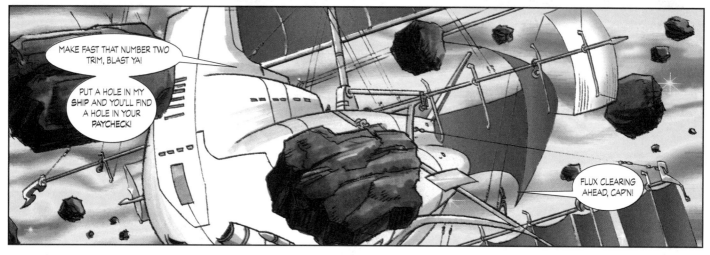

OKAY, HERE WE ARE. NOW HOW DO WE FIND HELP LOOKING FOR ROSS?

LET'S ASK ONE OF THE CENTRANS.

EXCUSE ME. WE'RE LOOKING FOR A FRIEND OF OURS WHO IS MISSING. IS THERE SOMEONE WHO COULD HELP US?

TRY THE CORPORATE POLICE. THEY HAVE A MISSING PERSONS OFFICE IN THE CORPORATE GOVERNMENT BUILDING.

AH. AND WHERE WOULD WE FIND THAT?

DON'T KNOW YOUR WAY AROUND, EH? YOU MUST COME FROM OFF-CENTER.

I BET YOU'RE HERE TO WATCH THE RECLAMATOR LAUNCHING!

WE'LL NEVER SEE ANYTHING LIKE IT AGAIN. A WHOLE NEW AGE, BEGINNING RIGHT IN FRONT OF OUR EYES!

IT'LL BE A PROUD MOMENT! NOT JUST FOR THE CENTER, BUT FOR ALL THE CORE WORLDS!

ANYWAY, THE CORPORATE HEADQUARTERS ARE IN THAT BIG RED BUILDING IN DEREGULATION PLAZA. JUST FOLLOW FREEMARKET STREET. YOU CAN'T MISS IT.

THE GUARD ROBS AT THE FRONT DOOR WILL DIRECT YOU TO THE POLICE OFFICE.

MAYBE WE SHOULD ADVERTISE FOR HIM. THAT SEEMS TO BE THE CENTRAN WAY.

WE'D BETTER BE PREPARED FOR A LONG SEARCH.

!

UH...MAYBE NOT.

He came from another world...

to solve the problem you never knew you had!

HAIR FOR LIFE

INTERACT!

?!

HE CAME FROM A UNIVERSE AWAY...FROM A WORLD OF PROGRESS— BUSINESS— MIRACLES OF TECHNOLOGY!

HE CAME TO SHARE HIS PLANET'S MIRACLES WITH OUR WORLD...AND TO ENRICH THE LIFE OF EACH AND EVERY CENTRAN!

FROM HIS EXECUTIVE SUITE HIGH ATOP THE CORPORATE GOVERNMENT HEADQUARTERS, ROSS McHUGH WORKS TIRELESSLY TO BRING YOU, HIS NEW FRIENDS, RELIEF...

...RELIEF FROM THE PROBLEM YOU NEVER KNEW YOU HAD...

BALDNESS!

HI, I'M ROSS McHUGH—AND I'M HERE TODAY SO YOU CAN HAVE HAIR TOMORROW!

I GUESS WE WON'T HAVE TO RESCUE ROSS AFTER ALL...

NO...

WHAT'S HAIR, YOU MAY ASK. HAVEN'T CENTRANS BEEN HAIRLESS FOREVER? ISN'T THAT THE WAY IT'S MEANT TO BE?

...IF ANYTHING, WE MAY HAVE TO RESCUE THE CENTRANS FROM HIM!

JUST GIVE ME A MOMENT OF YOUR TIME. LET ME SHOW YOU SOME OF THE ADVANTAGES OF HAIR...THEN LET ME TELL YOU HOW YOU CAN HAVE A RICH, BEAUTIFUL HEAD OF HAIR ALL YOUR OWN!

PLEASE STATE BUSINESS.

WE'RE HERE TO SEE ROSS McHUGH.

YOU ARE COMING TO THE RECLAMATOR LAUNCH, AREN'T YOU, ROSS? WE'D LOVE TO HAVE YOU AS A GUEST OF THE CORPORATE GOVERNMENT.

ARE YOU KIDDING? I WOULDN'T MISS IT!

VICE-CHAIR McHUGH, THESE PERSONS WISH TO SEE YOU.

HUH? KIDS WEARING EARTH CLOTHES!

WAIT A MINUTE! I KNOW THAT BOY FROM SOMEWHERE! AND ISN'T THAT GIRL—

ULP!

HAVE THE GUARD ROBS BRING THEM UP! I WANT TO TALK TO THEM—IN PRIVATE!

THAT'S EASY. ROSS IS AN OPPORTUNISTIC BRAT.

HE'S SET UP A LITTLE KINGDOM AND HE'S AFRAID WE'LL WRECK IT.

ROSS SEEMS TO BE VERY IMPORTANT HERE. I WONDER WHAT HE'LL DO WITH US.

I NEVER ASKED THEM TO FOLLOW ME HERE.

AS LONG I'M THE ONLY EARTHLING IN THE CENTER, I'VE GOT A COMPETITIVE EDGE.

WITH THEM AROUND, I'M JUST ONE OF THE ALIEN CROWD.

BESIDES, I HAVE A PLACE HERE. THE CENTRANS RESPECT ME. THOSE KIDS WOULD JUST MESS THINGS UP.

I DON'T OWE THEM ANYTHING.

THEY'RE ALL PHONIES ANYWAY! THAT MEXICAN GIRL ISN'T ANY RICH KID.

AND THE FRENCH GUY ISN'T EVEN A GUY!

I'VE GOT A GOOD THING GOING HERE. THAT'S WHAT COUNTS.

IF THOSE GUYS WERE SMART ENOUGH TO FIND ME, THEY'RE SMART ENOUGH TO FIND THEIR WAY BACK TO EARTH.

THEY DON'T NEED ME.

VICE-CHAIR McHUGH, THE LIGHTS ARE DIMMING FOR ARTIFICIAL HUMAN "NIGHT" PERIOD.

LEAVE ME ALONE!

VELOCITY OF HURLED OBJECT 38% TOO SLOW TO EFFECT BREAKAGE OF UNIT. SUGGEST HEAVIER OBJECT.

OH, SHUT UP.

THE GREAT MOMENT ARRIVES! THE ENTIRE CENTER TURNS OUT FOR THE RECLAMATOR LAUNCH...

ARE YOU SURE YOU WANT TO INTERROGATE THE PRISONERS NOW, ROSS? IT'S ALMOST TIME FOR THE CEREMONY.

I'LL ONLY BE A MOMENT. THERE'S SOMETHING I NEED TO CLEAR UP.

IF IT ISN'T HIS HIGHNESS, KING ROSS.

LISTEN, GUYS, I'VE COME TO SAY I'M SORRY. I SHOULDN'T HAVE DONE THIS.

ALL MY LIFE I'VE WANTED TO BE IMPORTANT. BEING THE FIRST ALIEN HERE MADE ME IMPORTANT. REALLY IMPORTANT.

WHEN YOU GUYS SHOWED UP, I GOT SCARED. ALL I THOUGHT OF WAS HOW I COULD LOSE EVERYTHING I HAD.

ON THE INTERNET YOU WERE SO KIND. YOU CARED FOR EVERYONE. YOU ALWAYS KNEW WHAT TO SAY TO HELP SOMEONE OUT.

AW, I GOT ALL THAT STUFF FROM BOOKS AND OFF CD-ROMS. WHAT YOU SAW IN MY OFFICE WAS THE REAL ME, NOT MY CLIP-ART PERSONALITY.

LOOK, I CAN MAKE IT UP TO YOU.

THE PRESIDENT'S TAKING ME TO THE RECLAMATOR LAUNCH NOW. AFTERWARD, I'LL COOK UP SOME STORY TO GET HER TO LET YOU GO.

JUST WHAT IS THIS RECLAMATOR EVERYONE IS TALKING ABOUT?

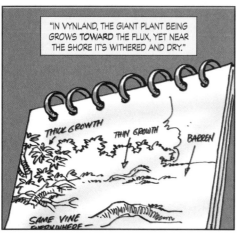

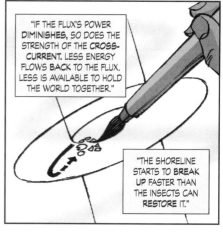

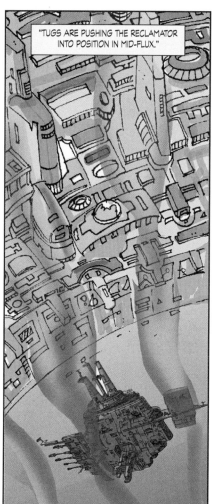

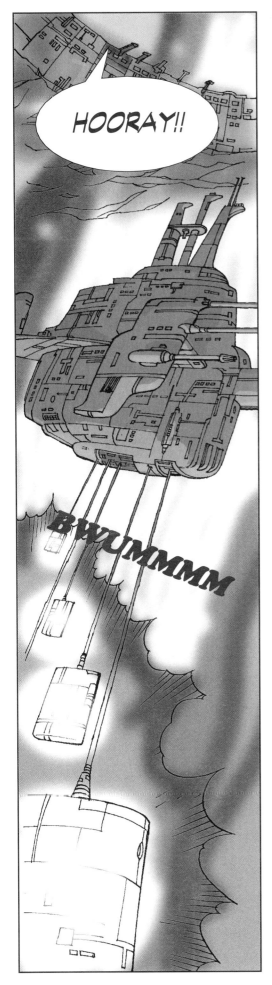

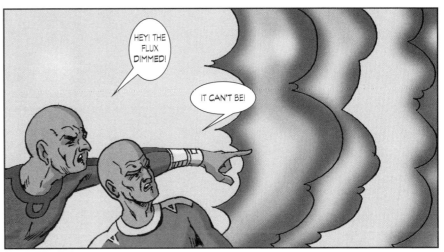

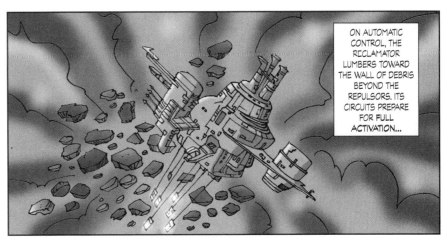

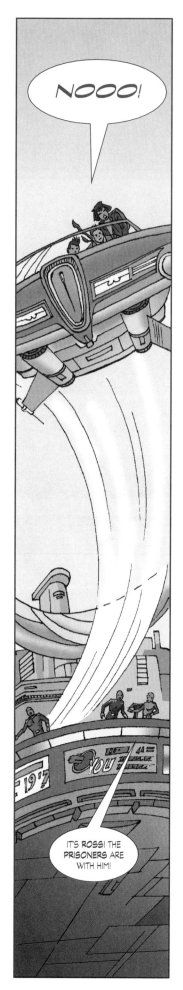

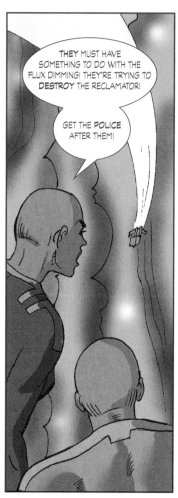

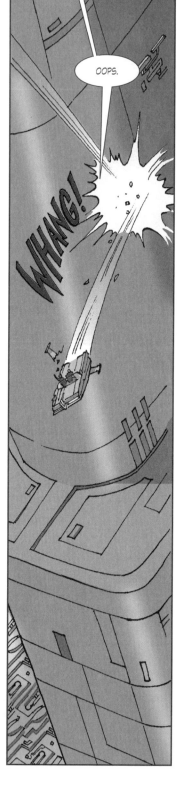

MAYBE WE CAN SMASH ENOUGH STUFF TO SHUT IT DOWN!

THERE'S MILES OF STUFF TO SMASH!

ROSS, I NEED YOUR COMPUTER.

I CAN BRUISE A FEW CIRCUITS WITH THIS THING!

GABRIELA, USE SOMETHING FROM YOUR TOOL BELT!

I'M TRYING, BUT I DON''T KNOW WHERE TO START!

TARO, WHY ARE YOU JUST SITTING THERE?

WHAT CAN BE TURNED ON...

...CAN BE TURNED OFF.

!!!

PROUD PEOPLE LIKE THE CENTRANS LOVE TO DOCUMENT THEIR ACCOMPLISHMENTS.

I LOOKED UP WHERE TO FIND THE POWER SWITCH.

THE TERRORISTS HAVE SABOTAGED THE RECLAMATOR!

BUT LOOK! THE FLUX BRIGHTENED WHEN THE RECLAMATOR SHUT DOWN!

THIS IS THE POLICE!

WE HAVE YOU SURROUNDED!

ROSS, TARO, CLAUDE, GABRIELA, WE OWE YOU A **GREAT DEBT**.

YOU KEPT US FROM MAKING A **DEADLY** MISTAKE.

YOU WERE **TOO CLOSE TO** THE PROBLEM. YOU KEPT DEVELOPING NEW TECHNOLOGY TO **FIGHT** IT WITHOUT STEPPING BACK TO SEE THAT THE TECHNOLOGY **ITSELF** WAS AT FAULT.

WHAT MUST WE DO TO **REPAIR** THE DAMAGE WE'VE DONE?

IN A WAY, YOU MUST DO **NOTHING**. STOP WEAKENING THE CORE WORLDS WITH YOUR COLLECTORS, AND THE **INSECTS** WILL EVENTUALLY REBUILD THE LAND.

IT WILL **TAKE** A WHILE...

CENTRANS DON'T TAKE WELL TO DOING NOTHING.

PASSIVE TECHNOLOGY LIKE THE BLEAKER **POWER WHEELS** MAY PROVIDE MOST OF THE ENERGY THE CENTER NEEDS...

...BUT YOU'LL STILL HAVE TO GET USED TO A LOWER STANDARD OF LIVING.

CENTRANS DON'T TAKE WELL TO LOWERED STANDARDS OF LIVING.

LUCKILY, CENTRANS DON'T TAKE WELL TO HAVING THEIR WORLD **FALL APART** UNDER THEIR FEET.

YOU'RE **CLEVER** PEOPLE. YOU'LL FIGURE IT OUT IF YOU WORK TOGETHER. YOU'LL PROBABLY EVEN FIGURE OUT A WAY TO MAKE A **PROFIT**.

LATER...

WE MAY HAVE MADE IT POSSIBLE FOR THE CORE WORLDS TO **REUNITE**. THE **HARMONIZER** WILL HAVE COMPANY AT LAST.

THIS TIME THE CENTRANS MIGHT WORK **WITH** THE OTHER WORLDS AND FIND WAYS THAT'LL BENEFIT **EVERYONE**.

THE CORE WORLDS CAN ACCOMPLISH A LOT TOGETHER.

SO CAN **WE**.

THE END!

What is the INTERNET?

You guys may not be able to visit other worlds through your computer monitor...but you can have fun exploring *this* world through the *Internet!*

The Internet is a *global network* which can connect *your* computer with *others* all around the world.

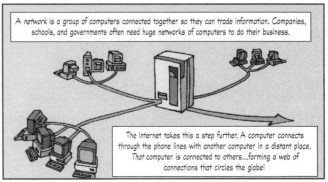

A *network* is a group of computers connected together so they can trade information. Companies, schools, and governments often need huge networks of computers to do their business.

The Internet takes this a step further. A computer connects through the phone lines with another computer in a distant place. *That* computer is connected to others...forming a web of connections that circles the globe!

During the "Cold War" between America and the Soviet Union, the U.S. government laid the foundation for the Internet. To make it easier to exchange information between military facilities and universities doing government research, the U.S. built a network connecting five *supercomputer centers* in different parts of the country. This "backbone" network is run by the National Science Foundation.

$e = mc...uh...hmm...?$

$1 + 1 = ?$

Over time, government branches and universities developed regional networks that connected to the NSF backbone. The Internet began to grow as local users connected to the larger net through these regional servers. The Internet was never run by one institution...it's a loose "club" of many separate groups, all agreeing to use the same computer language and communication rules, called *protocols*.

You don't need a special kind of computer to connect to the Internet. You do need a *modem* to hook your computer to the phone line, the proper software to "speak" the Internet language, and a *service provider* with an Internet connection.

Modem

World

The service provider can be something like a local *bulletin board service (BBS)* or one of the commercial *on-line services* like Compuserve or America Online. The provider charges you a fee to hook up.

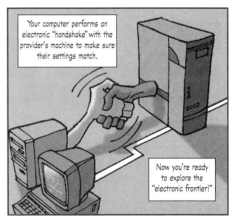

Your computer performs an electronic "handshake" with the provider's machine to make sure their settings match.

Now you're ready to explore the "electronic frontier!"

We're off for a drive on that "information superhighway" you keep hearing about!

HOSPITAL

UNIVERSITY

TO EUROPE

CORPORATION

NASA

TO ASIA

LIBRARY

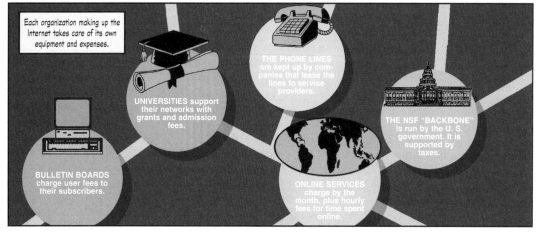

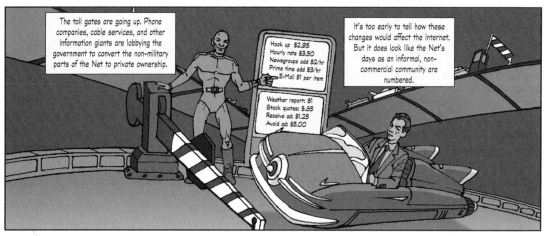